BELLA AND THE VAMPIRE

**TAKE ANOTHER TRIP
TO SHIVER-BY-THE-SEA:**

2: THE WERE-WOOF

ERIN DIONNE

ILLUSTRATED BY
JENN HARNEY

PIXEL✛INK

PIXEL✣INK

Pixel+Ink is an imprint of TGM Development Corp.
www.pixelandinkbooks.com
Printed and bound in June 2023 at Maple Press, York, PA, U.S.A.
Series book design by Kerry Martin
Interior book design by Jessica Nevins

Library of Congress Cataloging-in-Publication Data

Names: Dionne, Erin, 1975- author. | Harney, Jenn, illustrator.
Title: Bella and the vampire / Erin Dionne ; illustrated by Jenn
Harney. | Description: First edition. | New York : Pixel+Ink, [2023]
Series: Shiver-by-the-sea ; 1 | Audience: Ages 7-9.
Audience: Grades 2-3. | Summary: After moving to small, spooky
Massachusetts beach town Shiver-by-the-Sea, Bella Gosi must
team up with her new friend to help a kid vampire find
his way home.
Identifiers: LCCN 2023012676 | ISBN 9781645951674 (hardcover)
Subjects: CYAC: Friendship–Fiction. | Cities and towns–Fiction.
Vampires–Fiction.
Classification: LCC PZ7.D6216 Be 2023 | DDC [Fic]–dc23
LC record available at https://lccn.loc.gov/2023012676

Hardcover ISBN: 978-1-64595-167-4
E-book ISBN: 978-1-64595-168-1

First Edition

1 3 5 7 9 10 8 6 4 2

With deep thanks to John Bellairs's spooky
stories, which inspired my own
—E.D.

For Kelly and her café
—J.H.

CONTENTS

CHAPTER 1

The Beginning

THE full moon cast silver light onto the nearly empty Main Street below.

A group of boys laughed, jostling one another as they walked down the sidewalk. They paused in front of the old movie theater.

Grime smeared the ticket window, and instead of colorful movie posters, cracked, empty frames advertised dirt and cobwebs.

But a bright white sign hung on one of the doors.

"'Under new management,'" one kid read. "Who's gonna want to see a movie in–"

"*Oooooo!*" High-pitched and warbly, the sound made them cringe.

"Hey, what the–"

The sound came again. "*Ooooooooo!*"

"Who's messing around? DeShawn?"

The tallest of the bunch shook his head. "Not me."

Just then, a yellowish light flickered deep behind the dirty ticket window.

THUMP!

"*Ooooooooo!*" The theater doors rattled, like something was trying to get out.

That was enough for the boys. They took off, feet pounding the pavement to get far away from the theater.

"*Ooooooooo!*" echoed eerily behind them.

CHAPTER 2

Just Enough Magic

THE town Bella Gosi was moving to was strange. The name was strange: Shiver-by-the-Sea. The school mascot was strange: the Chills. Main Street was strange: it was empty and quiet. Even more strange? Her mom seemed to think Shiver-by-the-Sea was *magical*.

"Shiver-by-the-Sea is a special place, Bella. You'll see."

As she stared out the window, Bella rolled her eyes.

Shiver-by-the-Sea did not look magical, or special, in the least. The buildings seemed gray and sad.

The whole *town* seemed gray and sad.

"Magic should sparkle and be bright," Bella told her mom. "I don't see any magic here." They got out of the car in front of the movie theater. *Their* movie theater. Earlier in the summer, Bella's mom bought the theater and was planning to reopen it. That's why they were here. Well, that and other reasons, like her parents had decided not to live together anymore, which meant Bella's dad and her best friends were still in New York City.

"It's rusty movie magic. We're going to clean it off and shine it up," her mom said.

The building *definitely* needed a cleaning. The dirt darkening the ticket window and the empty frames sent a creepy tingle down Bella's spine. *It's just a building*, she reminded herself.

"And speaking of magic . . . ," her mom said, pointing.

Bella turned. Uncle Van headed toward them, holding a big bag of potato chips.

Bella ran over and hugged him tight.

"Hold these," he said, handing her the potato chips—pickle 'n' pepper flavor. *Gross*. Then *SNAP!* went his fingers and a bright pink tissue paper flower appeared out of thin air. He passed it to her with a bow.

Bella grinned. Maybe Uncle Van would teach her some magic tricks, since she and her mom would be living with him.

"I figured your mom would want to look around the theater for a while, so I brought us a snack," he said. "I'm going to help her unlock the doors. Be right back." Uncle Van and her mom disappeared inside. No way was Bella going to follow them.

FLOOMPH!

Something furry crashed into the backs of her legs. Surprised, she dropped the chips and flower.

A short-legged, droopy-eared brown-and-white

dog dragging a leash grabbed the bag. He shook his head, rattling the chips inside.

"Casper!" a voice yelled. "Casper! Drop it!"

Bella crouched to pick up the flower. A pair of beat-up blue sneakers, laces untied, stepped in front of her, followed by brown hands, which grabbed the dog's leash.

Bella stood.

"I'm so sorry," the kid said, wrestling the chips

away from the dog. "Casper loves pickle flavored." The tang of dill tickled Bella's nose as the bag split and chips poured all over the sidewalk. Casper dove into the pile, tail wagging happily.

"He can have them," Bella said. "Pickle chips are gross."

"I agree. You met Casper. And I'm Cooper," the kid said, wiping the dill chip powder off his hands. He adjusted his blue baseball cap, which read THE CHILLS in fancy lettering, surrounded by wavy white lines.

"I'm Bella." She took a breath. "My mom bought the theater. We're moving here."

Cooper whistled. "The theater? Really? Three of my brothers say it's haunted. One isn't sure."

Casper chomped the last of the chips and plopped down at Cooper's feet. Cooper leaned over and scratched behind the dog's ears.

"My mom says it's dusty and there are spiders, but I don't think she's seen any ghosts," Bella said, ignoring the creepy vibe the theater had given her earlier. "Anyway, this whole town looks haunted, if you ask me."

Cooper gave her a sad smile. "There used to be a lot of shops and stuff on this street, but when the Northville Mall opened, the shops went away. It's kind of like Shiver-by-the-Sea became a ghost."

Bella didn't want to start a new life in a ghost town with supposedly rusty magic. She wanted the busy streets in New York City, where she'd lived until that morning. She wanted to eat ice cream and laugh with Ilaria and Ana, twins who happened to be her best friends. She wanted her parents to be together.

But she was here now. Now, she had to explore a new town, and try to make new friends to laugh and eat ice cream with, and get used to living with just her mom and Uncle Van.

A heaviness settled near her heart. She sighed. She may as well start now. "I'm going to pick out the theater's first movie. Do you want to help?"

"Sure," Cooper said.

A few minutes later, Mom and Uncle Van staggered out to the small shady parking lot behind the theater, carrying a dusty trunk between them. They plunked the trunk down in front of Bella, who introduced Cooper. "You two can see what we've got. Find something good for opening night." Mom wiped her hands and stretched her back. "Thanks for helping, Cooper. You get a free ticket to our first show!"

Then she nudged Bella and loud-whispered, "Look at you, making friends *already*."

Bella's ears got hot.

Cooper grinned.

He crossed the lot and looped the leash over the fence, then poured some water from a bottle into a collapsible dog bowl. Casper slurped, then plopped to the ground and closed his eyes.

Meanwhile, Bella wiped the latches of the dusty trunk with a napkin. "How do we open it?"

Cooper studied the lid. "I think you have to slide

these pieces over, and the latch releases. You take that side."

Bella and Cooper each pushed on a latch. They clicked open, sending dust into the bright afternoon air. Bella sneezed.

Cooper stepped away from the trunk. "You do it," he said. "It's your movie theater."

Bella lifted the lid. It opened with a *crrreak,*

followed by a musty and plasticky smell. A jumble of round tins with white labels filled the trunk.

"What are those?" Cooper asked.

"Movies! They used to be on rolls of film and kept in containers. My mom taught me all about it." Bella pulled out a tin. "*Alligator People*. Reel one," she read off the label.

"'Reel one'?"

"That's what they called the roll of film. Lots of movies were too long to fit on one reel," Bella explained. "They were numbered so the person running the projector knew which order to show them in."

"That's pretty cool," Cooper said.

"We should match all of the reels before we decide which movie to show." Bella grabbed a few tins and carefully placed them on the ground.

"Here's *Dracula!*" Cooper said, waving a tin.

"Everyone knows the name *Dracula*. Should that one be first?"

"Maybe. Uh . . . Bella?"

"What?" she asked, kneeling in front of the trunk to find the other *Dracula* reel.

"You may want to come out of there." Cooper's voice sounded a little funny to Bella—high and squeaky.

"Okay. Why?" Bella stood, brushed off her knees, and turned to him.

Cooper's eyes widened. He pointed. *"Eek!* In the l-lid!"

"Did you say 'eek'?" But Bella turned toward where he was pointing . . . at the furry brown crea-ture tucked into a corner of the trunk's lid.

"Eek!" she shrieked, stepping back in surprise. "Is that what I think it is?!"

CHAPTER 3

Eek!

COOPER pointed again. "It's a bat. You eeked, too!"

"I did," Bella admitted. "But it's just a bat. Not a monster. Hopefully, the little guy's okay."

"You—not scared of bats?" Cooper asked as Bella took off her hoodie and carefully wrapped the animal in it. Its wings fluttered against the fabric. "You could get rabies or some zombie disease."

"My dad and I volunteered at a wildlife sanc-tuary in the Bronx sometimes," Bella said, feeling a twinge of sadness for her old life. Would she be able to help animals here in Shiver-by-the-Sea? She cradled the tiny, sweatshirt-wrapped bat in her arms. "I really like animals."

Cooper cautiously peeked at the bundle. "It's probably thirsty. I would be if I were stuck in a trunk. What do bats drink?"

"Water," Bella answered. She carried the bat across the parking lot to Casper's dish. Casper seemed gentle, but to be on the safe side, she scooted the bowl farther away. When she lowered the little bat to drink, Casper's nose wrinkled and he sprang to his feet, barking loud and fast.

POP!

The sharp sound echoed in the afternoon air.

The little bat was *gone*—and a small, dark-haired boy wearing jeans and a red shirt knocked her right over. A lightning bolt of surprise zipped through Bella.

"I'm going to yell something other than eek!"
Cooper cried.

"*Don't!*" Bella shouted.

Cooper snapped his mouth closed, but Casper
kept barking.

The boy-who-was-a-bat stood in the shade of
the parking lot, blinking at them, looking very, *very*
startled.

"Hi," said Bella with a wave. She felt bad for the
boy. Or bat. Or whatever he was. Being pulled out of

a trunk and turning into something different must have been scary for him, too. She wondered if characters in fairy tales or movies felt the way she did right now: like the glue that held her world together wasn't sticking. She forced herself to sound calm. "We're not going to hurt you. Don't be scared, okay?"

"I'm scared," Cooper muttered, moving to Casper's side. The dog stopped barking, but they both seemed ready to run.

Bella crouched in front of the boy, pushing through the shock of his transformation. He looked like a regular kid, even if he had been a bat a few seconds before. A regular, scared kid. She understood that feeling. She gave him a small smile.

The boy cautiously returned the smile, then pointed at the water.

He *was* thirsty!

"Cooper, grab my water bottle," Bella said. "Please," she added when he didn't move.

Grumbling, he tugged Casper to the trunk, scooped up Bella's water bottle, and brought it back to her. Casper strained at his leash, tail down, pulling away from the strange boy.

Bella unscrewed the cap and handed it over. The boy took a big gulp, then spat the water out, almost splashing Bella's sneakers. He frowned at the bottle.

"That's not what you want?" Bella said, her heart beating fast. "You don't drink water?" If he didn't drink water, what *did* he drink?

Oh no, she thought, scrambling backward, the hot pavement digging into her hands.

The only creatures she'd heard of that started as bats and turned into people were . . .

"Vampires," she whispered.

CHAPTER 4

Are You a Vampire?

"**EXACTLY!**" Cooper shouted. "THAT'S WHY I'M OVER HERE!"

Bella scooted the rest of the way across the parking lot and stopped near Cooper and Casper. Her hands shook and her heart pounded so hard she couldn't catch her breath.

But then she looked at the boy again.

His eyes were wide and wet, like he was about to cry, and a frown turned the corners of his mouth down. He was definitely scared. He didn't *seem* dangerous. He seemed like the lost third grader who she brought to the right classroom on the first day of school last year. Still, she wasn't sure. What if this boy attacked, like a wild animal?

"Um . . . hi?" Bella called from the other side of the parking lot.

The boy cleared his throat. "Hello."

"Are you okay?" Bella asked, willing her heart to slow down and her voice to stay steady.

The boy shook his head.

"Why are you here?" Cooper blurted out.

The boy tilted his head, like he wasn't sure what Cooper meant.

Bella took a few steps closer. "Here, at the movie theater. Where's your home?"

"Far away." The boy spoke very quietly. "I am very thirsty," he added.

"I bet! You probably want to drink our blood!" Cooper cried. He hugged Casper tightly. The dog gave a sharp bark, like he agreed.

The boy smiled, flashing pointy teeth straight out of a scary movie. "You are silly. I do not drink blood."

"So what *do* you drink?" asked Bella, relief spreading through her body.

The boy frowned. "I do not know the word in English."

"But you *are* a . . ." Bella took a breath. "A vampire?"

The boy shrugged. "If that is what you call it."

Bella stepped closer. The director of the wild-life sanctuary always said, *When dealing with wild animals, you have to remember that they're scared, and that's why they bite.* She took another deep breath. "If you're gentle and show kindness, they'll respond to that," she murmured, finishing the director's statement out loud to gather her courage. Maybe vampires would, too?

"You're probably right," Cooper said. Bella hadn't realized he'd heard her. She flushed.

"Do you have a name?" Cooper asked the boy.

"Bram."

"Hi, Bram. I'm Cooper, and this is Bella. Do you . . . live . . . in the theater?" Cooper spoke to Bram like any other regular kid and she relaxed more, too.

"No, but yes. I do not want to live there." He went quiet, looking at the ground, then the sky. "But it is where I live for now."

Bella frowned. That didn't sound right. Plus, he was young—he looked younger than Cooper and her. He couldn't be alone-alone. "Do you have a family?" she asked.

"Yes," he said softly. "And I miss them."

"Do you want to go home?" Cooper asked.

Bram lifted his head. His mouth turned down like a lowercase *n* and his eyebrows went up high, nearly disappearing into his black hair. "Very much yes. Will you help me go to my family?"

CHAPTER 5

That's ... Massachusetts

BELLA crouched in the shadows with Bram.

"We can call them for you if you want."

Bram hung his head. "I . . . do not know the phone number. When we came here, I did not want to learn."

"I'm not sure how to help you get home if we don't know where you're from," Bella said softly. The scariness of meeting a kid who changed from a bat was wearing off. She knew how it felt to be out of place. And she couldn't imagine being away from her mom—or how she'd feel if she were lost and couldn't get back to her. It was bad enough missing her dad all the time, and she knew exactly where he was.

"We need a map," Cooper called. He tied Casper's leash to the fence and came closer. Bella took that as a good sign. "He could show us if we had a map."

"Great idea!" Bella thought for a minute. "I'll be right back. Don't go anywhere," she said to Bram. She hoped Cooper would stick around, too.

She ran around the outside of the building to her mom's car. *Please be unlocked.* Mom always forgot to lock the door.

Bella grinned when the door swung open, then climbed into the back seat and rummaged through the bags and moving boxes. Not there.

Where did Mom pack it?

She turned and dug through some of the boxes in the hatchback. After a few minutes, she found it in a box labeled DESK. She slammed the car door behind her and raced back to the parking lot.

Sweaty and panting, she set the object in front of Bram—and Cooper, who'd moved even closer while she was gone.

"A globe?" Cooper asked.

"My mom has maps on her phone, but this was on our desk back home. It has all the world's countries marked on it."

Bram spun the globe on its stand. Bella expected his finger to touch down somewhere across the ocean.

"Here," he said. Cooper and Bella leaned closer. Bella furrowed her eyebrows.

"That's . . . Massachusetts," Cooper said, sounding disappointed. "It's where we are now." He and Bella exchanged a glance.

"That's not where I thought vampires were from," Bella added. They turned to Bram.

He shrugged.

"So, how did you end up in the trunk?" Bella asked.

Bram kicked at the pavement. "My family makes sweets."

"Like candy?" Cooper said.

Bram nodded. "We lived in Transylvania for a long time, but my parents' dream was to come to America and open a candy store. So we came here in the springtime." He was quiet for a minute. "I . . . did not want to leave my home."

Bella knew how that felt. She'd cried and cried when she said goodbye to her dad and her apartment in New York.

"It is loud here. And big. My parents picked out

a place for the store. I did not want to stay, so I decided to go back to Transylvania."

"All by yourself?! But that's so far away!" exclaimed Bella.

"It was so hard! I tried and got lost. So I found that building and hid. There is food and a dark place to sleep during the day. At night I was lonely, so I sang songs to keep myself company."

Cooper gasped. "You haunt the theater?"

"Haunt?"

"Make creepy noises and turn on lights at night."

Bram frowned. "Those are not creepy noises. They are my Transylvania songs!" Then he looked at his sneakers. "I tried to stay quiet, but I am afraid of the dark."

Vampires can be afraid of the dark? Bella clasped her hands in front of her heart.

This was turning into a very strange day.

"Can I talk to you for a minute?" Cooper asked Bella. She left the globe with Bram while she and Cooper huddled near where Casper was tied up.

The dog's eyes stayed focused on the vampire.

"Are you really thinking you'll help him get home?" Cooper said in a low voice.

"If you were lost, wouldn't you want someone to help you?"

"Yes, but he's a monster!" Cooper whispered.

Bella glanced at Bram over Cooper's shoulder. He was scraping a rock against the pavement.

"I'm pretty sure he's not a monster." But then again, Bella didn't think that Shiver-by-the-Sea was actually magic, and a bat who turned into a kid was not not-magical. She furrowed her eyebrows. "Look, I'm going to figure this out. Will you and Casper help me?"

Cooper kicked the ground. Bella held her breath, waiting.

"Okay. We'll help. Even though I'm still kind of scared of him."

Bella offered a hand for a high five. Cooper smacked it. "Let's go tell him."

Bram looked up when they got closer.

Bella gave him a cheek-stretching smile. "We need to know what you eat, and then we're going to help you get home."

Bram grinned, showing all of his pointy teeth again. Cooper gulped.

"Thank you very much," the vampire boy said.

"But first," Bella said, "we have to clean up this mess."

CHAPTER 6

Sweet Stuff

BELLA and Cooper quickly packed the reels in the trunk. They kept *Dracula* out as their pick for the theater's first movie.

"Seems like the best choice," Cooper said with a grin.

Bram stayed in the shade of the tree. He fanned himself, like he was trying to cool off.

"We need to get him something to drink," Bella said to Cooper once they snapped the giant trunk's latches.

"But what?"

"Bram, what did you eat while you were in the theater?" Bella asked. She guessed it hadn't been popcorn. He leaned against the fence at the edge of the parking lot with his eyes closed. *He really doesn't look good*, she thought.

"Sweet. In big bottles," he muttered, not opening his eyes. "The sun—it makes me too tired."

"I didn't think vampires could *be* in the sun," Cooper said to Bella in a low voice. "Without, you know . . ." He grimaced and stuck his tongue out.

"I can hear you," Bram said from his spot against the fence. "The sun takes my energy away fast. It can make me sick, but not—" He made the same face as Cooper, then went back to fanning himself.

Bella giggled. Okay, Bram needed a cold, sweet drink. "You drink sweet stuff?" she asked. "Like lemonade?"

Bram gave a weak nod.

They didn't have anything like that in the parking lot, and Bella couldn't exactly ask her mom for big bottles of soda for the vampire kid outside.

Cooper snapped his fingers. "I've got an idea. I'll be right back." He grabbed Casper's leash and the two of them raced around the building, Casper's long ears swinging as he loped.

"Do you feel okay?" Bella asked, turning back to Bram. He shook his head.

"It's hard . . . to be like this . . . when I'm thirsty."

"Hard to be . . . a boy?"

He nodded.

If it was harder for him to be a boy . . . "Can you change back into a bat?" she asked, then gulped at the thought.

Bram tilted his head. "Not . . . scary?" he asked.

"Maybe a little. But if it makes you feel better, go for it."

Bram gave her a friendlier smile, one without all the pointy teeth.

Just as before, there was a loud *POP!* and then instead of Bram sitting next to her, on top of her hoodie rested a small, furry brown bat. The little Bram-bat closed his eyes and fell asleep in a matter of seconds.

The back door of the theater swung open. Bella's mom came out.

So much for your nap, Bram. Bella scooped up Bram-bat and the sweatshirt and tucked the bundle in her lap.

"How'd it go?" Bella's mom asked. The cobwebs and dust on her clothes were visible from where Bella was sitting.

"Fine!" Bella called. "I'm going to stay over here so I don't sneeze." *And so you don't see the vampire kid we found in the trunk.* "We picked *Dracula* for the first movie."

"Great!" Mom said, moving closer. She opened

a bottle of water and took a long drink. "Where's Cooper? And his dog? And why is the globe out here?"

"I showed Cooper where we used to live. Then they . . . ran to get something."

"I got it! I got it!" Cooper shouted, red-faced and panting, as he and Casper came around the side of the building, a big grocery bag in his hands. "I got so much stuff! Bram is going to—" He stopped as soon as he spotted Bella's mom. "Oh, hi," he said, tucking the bag behind his back. Casper sniffed at it, tail wagging.

"Bella told me you two were finished." Bella's mom checked her watch, then glanced at Bella. "I bet you're ready to go to Uncle Van's and see the house. I'll wrap up here soon. The inspector left. We can open!"

"That's awesome!" Bella wanted to run over and high-five her mom, but stayed put with Bram-bat. "I'm so excited. Take your time doing whatever you have to do." Ms. Blackstone grabbed a handle at one end of the trunk and pulled, dragging the heavy box to the theater.

"Where's Bram?" Cooper asked, frowning.

Bella pointed to her lap.

Cooper gasped. "He . . . turned again?"

"It's hard for him to be a kid when he's hungry. What did you get?"

"Oh, yeah. Look!" Cooper nudged Casper away from the bag, then opened it. Inside was the largest jumble of junk food Bella had ever seen. "I got it from my house. Well, from my brother's secret candy stash in his room."

"Won't he find out and get mad?" Bella had always kind of wanted a sibling, even though she'd be pretty mad if they took stuff from her room.

"There are six of us," Cooper explained. "Even if DeShawn notices, he'll never figure out it was me. I hope." He gulped.

Bella gently placed her sweatshirt and Bram on the ground in the shade. Then she and Cooper pulled out Pixy Pops, Lik-Kid Sugar, cans of soda, sugary sports drinks ("My mom never lets me have those," Bella said, awed), whipped cream, and—

"Maple syrup? Your brother keeps maple syrup in his room?"

Cooper laughed. "No! I got that and the whipped cream from the kitchen. They're sweet and drinkable, so I thought, why not try?"

Bella cradled Bram-bat in one arm. Cooper passed items to her and she held them for the bat to see. He gave a tiny head shake each time.

"This is not good," Bella said, putting the whipped cream down. "Maybe Bram *did* have the word wrong."

"I hope not," Cooper replied. He grabbed the syrup. "One last try."

Bella held the bottle in front of the bat. Bram's eyes barely flickered.

But then the tiny bat's nose twitched. And twitched again! His eyes and mouth opened wide.

"That's it!" cried Bella. "Hurry, hurry!" Bram-bat

wiggled in her hands, struggling to get to the bottle.

"The cap is sticky." Cooper pried at the red plastic, finally popping it open. The smell of maple syrup—waffles and weekend breakfasts—filled the air.

Bram-bat lunged for the bottle, but the syrup was far down the neck. He squeaked, clearly frustrated.

"Hey, we'll help," Bella said. Cooper grabbed Casper's water dish and dumped it out, then glugged in the syrup and set the bowl on the ground. Bella placed Bram-bat nearby.

He slurped the syrup like it was water.

Bella and Cooper cheered, then each opened a Pixy Pop to celebrate. They watched Bram-bat eat—or drink. When his belly was big and round and he was sleeping for real, Cooper turned to Bella.

"What are we going to do now?"

"He can't stay in the theater anymore. Mom's getting it ready to open. We have to bring him home."

"How will we find his family? He doesn't even know where they are." Cooper nudged Casper away from what was left of the maple syrup.

"We can do it," Bella insisted. Bram let out a bat-sized snore. "His parents are probably really worried about him, and he misses them."

The theater door opened. Uncle Van stuck his head out.

"I'm ready to pack it in, Bella," he called. "Your mom's almost done. Cooper, it was nice meeting you. We'll be here all weekend if you want to stop by again."

"I'll meet Mom around front," Bella said. She

turned to Cooper. "Can Bram stay with you while we figure out where he lives?"

"I can't take him home," Cooper said, folding his arms. "We have two cats, and they hate Casper. I'm sure they'd try to eat a syrup-filled bat."

Bella hadn't thought of cats. Did Uncle Van have one?

"Well, I guess I'll take him to Uncle Van's for tonight," she said. She hoped she could hide a bat-boy from her family in a house she hadn't been to in ages. "Then we can come up with a plan to get him home." She gathered the sticky bat in her now-sticky sweatshirt and patted Casper on the head. Cooper scribbled something on a piece ripped from the bag of sweets, then passed it to Bella. His address.

"Let's meet tomorrow," Cooper said, walking backward across the lot. Bella gave him a thumbs-up. Casper wagged his tail at her, then he and Cooper turned and headed down the sidewalk.

Bella adjusted the sweatshirt in her arms. As she walked around the corner to the car, she laughed to herself. This morning she had been worried about making friends in a new town. This afternoon, she'd made a new human friend, a new dog friend, *and* a new vampire friend.

Maybe this move wasn't going to be so bad after all.

CHAPTER 7

Living in a Magician's Trunk

UNCLE Van's house could have been straight out of a spooky old movie: it sat on top of a hill, and had wooden towers, round windows, and a big porch.

But it was also painted purple with bright pink trim, and flowers dotted the yard like sprinkles of confetti. A rainbow flag fluttered in the breeze, and smaller ones hung from the porch railing.

"Wow," Bella said.

Her mom laughed. "You were so little the last time we were here. I'm not surprised you forgot what it looked like." She pressed the button on an opener from Uncle Van, and the pointy fence gate swung out. Their car puttered through.

Bella glanced down at Bram-bat. Still asleep. She directed her attention out the car windows.

It was a short drive up the hill to the house. Peppered among the flowers were funny garden statues: gnomes standing on their heads, stone rabbits wearing top hats, ceramic frogs frozen mid-leap, and brightly colored mushrooms with polka dot caps.

"It's so cute!" Bella said, realizing she had a big grin on her face. Even though she missed her old familiar apartment, Uncle Van's garden and house made her feel warm, invited . . . and *happy*?

Happy, she decided.

She hadn't expected that.

Honestly, there was a lot about today that she hadn't expected.

Mom stopped the car. "Van says he likes to come home with a smile."

Bella gathered her sweatshirt, hoping to quickly find a Bram-bat hiding place.

They climbed the stairs to the porch and pressed the bell. Instead of a regular *ding-dong*, it played the first notes of "Twinkle, Twinkle, Little Star." Bella giggled. Her mom shook her head.

Uncle Van came to the door. His polka dots had been replaced by a Hawaiian shirt covered in giant colorful flowers.

"Trisha! Bella! You live here now. No need to ring. Use your key!" He reached out and pulled a shiny brass key from behind Bella's ear. Bella pocketed it, and he stepped back to let them in.

The room was like a museum, amusement park, and Hollywood props department all jumbled up: stage trunks served as tables, and everywhere Bella looked, there was something special—mannequins wearing hats, giant ostrich feathers, glittering mirrors, carvings and statues and tapestries, stuffed doves and trinkets. Uncle Van basically lived in a magician's trunk.

"Whoa," Bella said. In her excitement, she'd clutched Bram-bat rather tightly, and loosened her grip.

"Do you like it?" Uncle Van asked.

"It's amazing," Bella replied.

"It's something," her mom said with a laugh.

Van dropped into a deep bow, a top hat appearing in his hand. He straightened and tossed it on his head. "Everything comes from my travels and shows. But you can look at it all later. Let's get to your rooms!"

They climbed a crooked staircase into one of the towers, passing a stained-glass window. Sunlight sent red and blue and orange splotches across the walls and floor.

Uncle Van pushed the door at the top. "Here you go," he said, then stepped aside.

This room was the only one in the tower. It was round, with a wooden floor, a big bed on one side, and light blue wallpaper printed with clouds. On a soft round rug stood two bright pink chairs facing each other, an oval table between them. And there were birdcages. All types—wire ones, sturdy-looking bamboo ones, metal ones, tiny ones, big ones—placed around the room.

"I hope it's okay," Uncle Van said shyly. "I mean, I know you'll have to get used to it . . ."

"Yeah, it'll be pretty hard," Bella said with a very serious expression.

Panic flashed in Uncle Van's eyes.

"I'm kidding! I *love* it." She threw the arm not holding the bat around her uncle.

"I'll bring your things up," he said, the tips of his ears turning pink. "That way, you can get settled."

As soon as she heard her uncle's footsteps on the stairs, Bella placed her sweatshirt on the bed, then unwrapped it. Bram-bat was still asleep.

"Let's get you somewhere comfortable," she whispered.

She scanned the space. More than one birdcage would be big enough for Bram, but she couldn't lock him up. What would her mom or uncle say if they saw a caged bat in her room?

She'd have to hide him.

There were two more doors aside from the one entrance. One opened into a small, white-tiled bathroom. A shower curtain printed with peacock feathers wrapped around the claw-foot tub. She yanked the other, relieved to find a closet.

"Here you go, friend." She stood on tiptoe and tucked Bram-bat on the shelf in the back corner.

—◆—

I will get used to this, Bella thought as she settled into bed that night. Even though she was in a new house, the sky wallpaper made the room feel magical and cozy. Finding a way to get Bram home might be a challenge, but she and Cooper could do it together.

Her body relaxed, her eyes drooped closed, and then—

POP!

And "*OW!*"

Followed by *THUD*.

Bella jumped out of bed and ran to the closet, heart slamming.

Bram, boy-shaped, was sprawled on the closet floor looking very confused. "Where am I?" he asked.

"Shhhh!" Bella hissed. Footsteps pounded up her staircase.

"Bella?" Her mom's worried voice carried as she climbed. "Are you okay?"

Bella quickly closed the closet door on Bram and made it halfway to her bed before the other door opened.

Mom and Uncle Van stood there, concerned. Mom wore workout clothes, but Uncle Van had changed into blue pajamas dotted with sloths.

"I'm fine," Bella said, trying very hard not to look at the closet. "I . . . I fell out of bed." Her mom rushed to her side and hugged her, smoothing her hair.

"That's a pretty big fall," Uncle Van said. "Are you hurt?"

"N-no," she answered. "Mom! Too tight!"

Her mom released her grip and stepped back, eyeing her. "You sure you're okay?" she asked.

"Positive." *Please leave. Please leave, please leave.* "I guess I have to get used to the bed," she added, forcing a grin.

Her mom and uncle fussed a little more, then closed her door.

Bella waited until their footsteps thunked across the downstairs floor before she dared move.

She scurried over to the closet, throwing the door open.

"What happened?"

CHAPTER 8

POP!

BRAM lay curled on the floor, eyes wide. "I could not help it," he said. "I think it happened when I woke up. Where am I?"

Bella explained as they settled in the chairs. "You're safe here if you stay quiet."

"All right. But I am hungry."

Bella hadn't brought any maple syrup to her room, so she'd have to sneak a bottle from the kitchen.

"Can you wait a little bit?"

Bram frowned, but he nodded.

"How does turning into a bat feel?" Bella asked. "Does it hurt?"

Bram shook his head. "No, it happens fast. Like one minute I'm this way, and then–"

POP!

Bram-bat sat in the chair across from her.

POP!

Bram-the-kid again.

Bella put her finger to her lips, listening for footsteps.

None came. She relaxed. Bram sat, legs curled under him, picking at a spot on his jeans. Bella didn't understand how his clothes changed with him, but she thought it rude to ask.

"Thank you for helping me. It was"—he paused, like he was finding the right word—"lonely in the theater."

"I bet it was! How long did you live there?" As Bella pictured living alone in the dusty, dark theater, a shiver went down her spine. She understood why he'd been afraid at night. She'd be scared, too.

"Two weeks," Bram said. "One night, I wrote a note for my family. It said I was going back home to Transylvania. Then I turned into a bat and flew away. But there was a lot of—what is the word in English for clouds but on the ground?"

"Fog?"

"Yes. Fog. It is hard to fly in fog. I went lots of wrong ways. I got very tired and took a break and went to sleep. In the morning I saw the theater and smelled sweet stuff inside. So I found an open window, flew in, and had a drink. To sleep, I could turn into a bat and hide in the open trunk. I did not know how to find my family. I stayed there and hoped they would find me. Then your mom closed the lid, and you found me instead."

"I know how it feels to miss a place," Bella said, thinking of her apartment in New York, with its big, square window that opened onto the fire escape and Mrs. Gomez who lived downstairs and always cooked something yummy. Her heart ached for her old life and the way her family used to be, but she couldn't imagine running away from Shiver-by-the-Sea alone to go back there.

"I helped set up the store when we first got here in the spring," Bram continued, pulling Bella away from her thoughts. "But a month went by and I made no friends. My parents said I would meet children when school starts and the store opens, but that seemed a long time to wait. I was lonely."

He was quiet for a moment. "And now I miss my family. My father has his one hundred and fiftieth birthday in two days and I cannot find them. Maybe they left to find me in Transylvania, and I am here alone?" His eyes got shiny, like he was going to cry. Bella grabbed some tissues from the tiny bathroom, and then passed them to Bram. He blew his nose.

"I don't think they'd leave you here by yourself." Bella hugged her knees. "I know if I ran away, my mom would try to find me. I bet your family's looking for you." She paused, thinking of something to cheer him up. "Hey, maybe we can get you home in time for your dad's birthday! That would be a good surprise."

"That would be the *best* surprise," Bram said. "Drink now?"

Bella nodded, then crept to her bedroom door and peeked out. Everything seemed quiet.

"I'll be back with a snack." On tiptoe, she snuck down the stairs.

Bright moonlight streamed through the windows, turning Uncle Van's mirrors and collections an eerie, magical silver. Another step and *creak!* She froze, holding her breath. Her heartbeat pounded in her ears, but around her, the house was quiet. Mom and Uncle Van were definitely asleep. She exhaled, then as fast as she could, scurried the rest of the way to the kitchen.

In her old apartment, the kitchen only had five cabinets and Bella knew where everything was. Here, there were at least twice as many.

She opened the one closest to her—plates. Next was a jumble of glasses. One at her feet—pots and pans. Up high again—cans of tomatoes and corn and soup. Did Uncle Van even *buy* syrup? Maybe he'd finished a bottle that morning? *UGH.*

Bella copied Cooper and gathered anything thick and syrupy she could find: chocolate sauce, molasses, and something labeled HB FOOD—SIMPLE SYRUP, which she spotted in the back of the fridge.

She grabbed an empty box from a stack by the

back door and loaded everything, adding a cookie for herself. Then she headed upstairs, avoiding the creaky board in the living room.

Once in her room, she unpacked the bottles on the table. Bram's mouth stretched into a hungry grin, showing his fangs. A tingle of fear shot through Bella when she spotted them.

"Try this," she said, quickly spooning chocolate sauce into his mouth.

"Yuck!" he said, swallowing it with a deep frown.

Bella almost laughed—a kid thinking chocolate sauce tasted terrible? Instead, she handed him the next thing to try. And when that wasn't right, the next.

And the next.

"This one?" she said with a yawn. It was late, and she needed sleep. Bram didn't seem at all tired.

Well, he *had* napped all afternoon.

"This one! YUM!" he said. He slurped at the HB Food bottle and Bella nibbled her cookie.

When he finished, Bella sniffed at the opening: sweet, and whatever had been inside was clear and sticky. If it took a while to find Bram's home, she'd need to get more of this stuff—or more maple syrup.

"Perfect," she said, yawning again. "Now we can both get some sleep."

Bram agreed, then sat on the floor of her closet and *POP!*

"Tomorrow we'll figure out our plan," she murmured.

A tiny squeak of agreement came from the inside of her closet.

CHAPTER 9

The Mall?

BELLA, Bram, and Cooper sat on the steps outside of Cooper's house. Getting Bram away from Uncle Van's had been easy. Mom had left for the theater before Bella came downstairs, and Uncle Van was in the garden. He'd waved when Bella stuck her head out the kitchen window and yelled she was going to meet Cooper, then she and Bram jogged out the front door, down the driveway, and through the big gate.

The hot sun made Bram tired and way hungrier. Luckily, Cooper's house had a big tree that shaded the yard. Casper was curled under it, far away from Bram.

"Snack?" the young vampire asked hopefully.

"Talk first, food next," Cooper replied.

The house's bright blue door opened, and a woman dressed in pink hospital scrubs with Cooper's same wide smile came out. "I'm headed to work, honey," she said. She bent and kissed Cooper on the head. "DeShawn's in charge. He's playing a video game." She turned to Bella and Bram. "You must be Bella. Cooper told me all about you last night. Welcome to Shiver-by-the-Sea. And is this your . . . brother?"

"Oh, thank you. No," Bella answered. "Not my brother. This is Bram. He's ... uh ..."

"A foreign exchange student," Cooper jumped in quickly. "Staying in Shiver-by-the-Sea."

"How nice." Cooper's mom looked slightly skeptical. "Well, enjoy your time here. And welcome, Bella. We're happy you're here."

"Thanks," said Bella, but Cooper's mom was already slipping into her car. The three kids watched her pull away, and then Bella and Cooper turned to Bram.

"So?" Cooper asked.

"The house has trees. It is white and square—"

"Not helpful," Bella interrupted. They'd never find the house. "What about the store? You were talking about that last night."

"Lots of lights," Bram said, his eyes closed, as though picturing it in his head before saying it out loud. Bella and Cooper exchanged a glance.

"So it's a big store?" Cooper tried.

"No." Bram shook his head and opened his eyes.

"Store is small, but it is in a big place. There is a water spray. Inside."

"Water spray?" Bella furrowed her eyebrows.

"I think he means a fountain," Cooper explained.

Bram nodded and clapped his hands. "Yes. That is the word. Fountain."

"Wait! The mall!" Cooper cried, jumping up. Casper raised his head and woofed in agreement. "The store is in the mall!"

"Yes!"

"Is it close by? Can we walk there?" Bella asked. She remembered seeing a mall on the drive into Shiver-by-the-Sea but had no idea where it was.

Cooper tilted his head. "It's pretty far to walk. . . . Do you have a bike? We could maybe ride over. I've never gone there by myself."

Bella frowned. She didn't have a bike. She'd never learned to ride one in New York. She and her mom took the subway everywhere. And Cooper said it was far. "I have a scooter. Maybe I could use that. What about Bram? How will we bring him with us?" They turned to him.

"I can walk," he said.

A long walk, plus bright sun, plus a hungry vampire seemed like a bad idea to Bella. They'd have to transport him.

"You could . . . ride in my bike basket," Cooper said slowly, almost as if reading Bella's mind. "But you'd have to be . . . small."

"A bat?" Bram asked.

Cooper gulped and nodded. "Yeah."

"I can do that!"

POP!

Cooper jumped. So did Casper, who barked sharply.

Bram-bat fluttered at eye level.

"Not during the day on my front lawn!" Cooper cried. He grabbed Casper's collar and calmed him down with pets and soft words.

POP!

Bram-the-boy stood there, grinning.

Casper let out one more woof, as if to say, "Not funny," before flopping onto the grass, exhausted.

Bella giggled. "Okay, so we'll take my scooter and your bike, and Bram gets a ride. I think my scooter's still in my mom's car, so we'll have to go to the theater to get it."

"To the theater!" Cooper called in a deep, movie voice.

"To the theater!" Bella and Bram echoed.

CHAPTER 10

Dumpster Diving

"**No,**" Bella's mom repeated. "You're not going anywhere."

Bella stood, arms crossed. Their "discussion" was happening in the lobby of the theater. A short, round vacuum was parked between them. Cooper, Casper, and Bram waited in the parking lot out back.

"Mom! It's important."

"Lots of things are important. It's almost lunchtime, and I still need help getting this place in order. Besides, the mall's not right around the corner. I'm not sure you should go by yourselves." She crossed her arms, copying Bella. "But if you keep pushing, I'll say you can't go at all."

"Finnnnne," Bella said, drawing out the word. "I'll

help. But what about Cooper and our new friend Bram and Casper?"

"They can help, too. The more the merrier."

———◆———

Bella went outside to fill in the others. Cooper sat in the shade scratching Casper's ears. "Where's Bram?" she asked.

Cooper pointed to the dumpster. "In there."

"What?" Bella screeched.

"Right before you came out, he said he smelled something tasty, then dove in. I was not going to investigate."

Bella rushed across the parking lot to the big boxy trash container. Patches of rust dotted the green paint, and WASTE REMOVAL and a phone number were stenciled on the side in big white type. "Bram? Hey, Bram, what are you doing?" Bella called out. She pinched her nose shut.

Bram's head appeared in a window-like opening on one side of the container, a big smile on his face. "I found it!"

"Found what?" With her nose still held closed, Bella's voice sounded funny to her own ears.

"Food!" He held up a big white jug that looked like a gallon of milk. "I can pass to you?"

Bella reluctantly let go of her nose and reached for the container. Happily, the dumpster did not smell like stinky hot garbage—more like dust and dryness.

A heavy, sweet smell overpowered the rest as

Bram passed her the jug, labeled SYRUP CONCENTRATE. *Perfect for Bram,* she thought.

Once the very dusty vampire climbed out of the dumpster, Bella handed the jug back to him. She wiped her hands on her shorts and faced Cooper.

"My mom doesn't want us to go. She has stuff she wants me to do here." Bella didn't know if she should ask the others to stay and help.

"What stuff?" Bram asked. He popped the cap off the jug and drank from it like it was a giant water bottle.

A giant water bottle pulled from a big bucket of garbage! Bella thought. *Ewwww!*

"Cleaning and covering the ticket booth with paper," Bella said instead.

"You help me, I will help you," he said matter-of-factly.

"I've got no plans today," Cooper added. "Let's get this done."

CHAPTER 11

On Wheels

SOON, the windows in the ticket booth sparkled and were covered with brown paper. After the group ate lunch—well, Bella and Cooper ate, Bram glugged from his syrup jug—Bella's mom tasked them with sorting junk in the theater office. They found movie posters, office supplies, flattened popcorn boxes, and ticket rolls.

By the time they finished, it was late afternoon.

"You worked so hard, I think you've earned a reward," Bella's mom said. She fetched her bag and pulled out a ten-dollar bill. "Get a treat, but not at the mall, okay? I think it's too far."

"Thanks, Mom!" Bella said. In New York, she'd been allowed to take the subway by herself to lots of places, as long as she was with a friend. Shiver-by-the-Sea was so much smaller. Why couldn't she go to the mall with Cooper and Bram? She folded the money and slipped it into her pocket, frowning. She didn't like disobeying her mom, but this was serious. They needed to get Bram home.

"While you're on Main Street, do me another favor?" her mom asked.

Bella groaned. Casper, lying on the floor under the desk, rolled onto his back.

"Sure," Bella said. "What do you need?"

"See if there's a place that might want to sell concessions here at the theater?"

"*Concessions?*" Bella repeated.

"Yeah—candy, popcorn—the stuff people eat at the movies."

"Okay," Bella said doubtfully, then she left to get her scooter from the car.

While she did that, Cooper brought Casper home and got his bike. Bram happily waited on the curb, glugging syrup from the jug.

"Don't finish it all," Bella said. How could one kid drink so much goo?

Bram slurped a big mouthful, then smiled at her, showing his fangs. "Why not? Soon I will be home and have all the food I need." He slurped again, but then stopped. The jug had been more than half full when he found it in the dumpster. Now, there was maybe a quarter left. He set it down.

Right then, Cooper came around the corner on a beat-up silver bike with a big front basket. "Two of my brothers had this before me," he explained, "but the basket's from when Casper was a puppy. I used to ride him around, so I'm good with passengers."

POP!

Bram was gone, but Bram-bat fluttered in his place. Bella tucked her hoodie into the basket and Bram-bat flew over. He grabbed the edge of the basket with his feet and stood there, looking down into the pile of sweatshirt.

"Oh! You need help," Bella said. She wrapped her hands around his tiny bat body and gently placed him in the basket. "Are you ready?"

Bram-bat squeaked and nodded.

"Let's go!" Bella said. She buckled her helmet under her chin.

"Where to?" Cooper asked.

"The mall."

"But your mom said no."

Bella frowned. "I know, but my dad always says that doing the right thing isn't always the easiest thing. Getting in some trouble is worth it if we can get Bram home."

She hoped she wouldn't get in trouble at all.

They zipped through downtown Shiver-by-the-Sea, Cooper pedaling while Bella scooted beside him. Bram peeked over the top of the basket. Soon the stores were behind them. The traffic noise quieted, replaced by seagull cries. The group carefully crossed a busy intersection, shaded by a big highway overpass. Bella recognized it from the ride into town with her mom.

"We don't have to go up there, do we?" she called nervously. There was a sudden gust of wind and clouds rolled across the sky, blocking the sun.

"No!" Cooper yelled over his shoulder. "We go under it!"

The ride was a lot farther than Bella expected. Her legs ached, and she wasn't so sure that this trip had been a good idea. Just as she was about to tell Cooper they should turn around, she spotted a sign—NORTHVILLE MALL—with an arrow pointing straight ahead.

They cruised beneath the dark, cool overpass, crossed to the other side, down a hill, and then Bella saw it: the mall.

CHAPTER 12

Lights Out

NORTHVILLE Mall was like any other mall: a huge building with glittery glass along the roof, surrounded by a moat of parking lots. Bella felt a thrill even looking at it. They were going to get Bram home!

As they coasted down the hill, though, something wasn't right.

"Why are all the cars leaving?" Bella asked. A sinking feeling crept into her stomach.

Cooper glanced over his shoulder. "I don't know. Maybe people going home for dinner?"

They got closer. People streamed out the doors. There were so many cars leaving, the pair had to be extra careful to avoid the traffic.

They crossed the big lot, zipped onto the sidewalk, and stopped at a bike rack. Cooper locked Bella's scooter, and she picked up the sweatshirt bundle with Bram. Then they headed toward the building.

A man wearing a blue uniform held the door open. MALL SECURITY was printed over his badge. "Sorry, kids. Mall's closed. You can't come in."

Bella's heart dropped. "Why?" she blurted.

"Power outage," the man said as he helped a mom lift her stroller onto the sidewalk. "Everything's closed."

Bella didn't want to look at the bat in her arms. She knew he could hear everything.

"When do you think the power will come back on?" she asked.

The security guard shrugged. "Probably tomorrow. The mall won't reopen today."

Bella spotted the defeated look on Cooper's face.

"We'll come back," she said for herself, for Cooper and Bram. "Let's go."

The return walk to the bike rack was quiet, and the ride home quieter, clouds darker. Bella's legs ached. This was a lot more scooting than she'd ever done in New York City.

The rain began as they came out from under the overpass.

"Oh great," Bella mumbled.

Worst. Day. Ever.

The rain stayed light, but they were still soaked by the time they reached the theater. Bram popped back into his kid form. He looked miserable, too.

"We'll go back tomorrow," Bella promised. "It will be your dad's birthday, and you'll be a big surprise gift. And it won't be raining." She shivered.

"Exactly," Cooper added, but he sounded tired, not excited.

The rain fell harder, and they pressed up against the building.

Bram sighed and picked up the almost-empty jug of syrup. "You were right, Bella. I should not have had so much syrup." He took a small sip and gave them a half smile. "I sleep in the closet tonight. We try again tomorrow."

CHAPTER 13

Bad News

THEY met behind the theater the next day.

"Bad news," Cooper and Bella said at the same time.

"You first," offered Cooper.

Bella grimaced. "I think I got caught yesterday."

"You think you did?"

"My mom didn't say anything, but I'm sure she knows what we did." She'd given Bella the Eyebrow as soon as she'd spotted Bella's sopping clothes. The Eyebrow meant, *I see that. I see you. I know things.* Bella had been on edge all night and this morning, waiting for a consequence, but her mom had gone back to the theater without another word. Bella shrugged. "Your turn."

Bram wandered to the edge of the dumpster, checking for more syrup.

"When I rode home last night, I must've hit something," Cooper said. "My back tire is flatter than a bookmark in a dictionary."

"Oh no!" A lump settled in Bella's stomach. "Can you get it fixed?" And then, to Bram, "Don't climb in there! Mom threw out a bunch of old nails." The boy-bat had one foot on the edge of the little window, ready to dive in.

Cooper raised an eyebrow.

Oh. That's how his tire had gone flat.

"My dad said he can fix it tonight—after work."

Bella groaned. "But that's too late for us to ride over. We'll have to come up with another way."

"Even though you may be in trouble?" Cooper asked crossing his arms.

"Even though. Is there a bus?"

"I think so," he said. "Only it's more like a . . . shuttle? People who are too old to drive take

83

it, I think. My grandma uses it to go to the grocery store." Bram walked over, holding his big container of syrup. What little was left sloshed around the bottom of the jug.

"If there's a shuttle, we can get there!" Bella said.

Cooper and Bram looked at her like she had five heads.

"What? I took public transportation all the time in New York," Bella said, ignoring the little twinge in her heart. "All you need is some money and a schedule. Where do you get the shuttle schedule?"

Cooper shrugged. "I don't really know. There's a sign on Main Street."

"Okay. Let's find it," Bella said. "I need to tell my mom where I'm going."

The theater wasn't quite ready for opening night, but it was getting close. The dark red carpets were clean, not dusty. A painted gold vine wound across the bright white walls instead of cobwebs.

On the other side of the room, Bella's mom

scrubbed the glass candy and popcorn counter. She waved. "Hey, kids!" She plopped a rag into a sudsy bucket. "What do you think?"

"Awesome," said Bella honestly. Her mom hadn't smiled like this in New York.

"Hello, Cooper," Ms. Blackstone said. "Hi, Bram."

The vampire leaned over the candy counter. "More syrup?"

Bella's mom laughed. "You mean from the soda machine? Can you even believe the last owners left that stuff here? I thought for sure the jugs would be covered in ants. I tossed them out back."

"Can we take the shuttle to the mall?" Bella asked.

Bella's mom crossed her arms. "Bella. *Really*?"

"Mom! I took the bus *and* the subway all the time with friends at home. In *New York City*."

"I know." Her mom sighed. "It's just that this is all new, and you've never done any of that *here* before ... *right*?" she said with extra emphasis.

Bella knew she knew. "Cooper, have *you* taken the shuttle to the mall?"

Standing behind her mother, Bella glared laser eyes in his direction.

"Um . . . yeah. Of course." He gulped. "All the time."

She sighed.

"Fine, then. I hope you didn't spend the money you earned yesterday. That's your fare."

"See you later!" Bella squeezed her mom. "I'll help you when we get back."

CHAPTER 14

The Bat on the Bus

THEY made the short walk to Main Street, sticking to the shade. There were a bunch of empty storefronts, but the library was open, and it had a cheerful rose garden out front. They passed a taco place called Chiles-by-the-Sea, a pizza shop, and a store with dark windows that appeared closed. As Bella got closer, she realized it wasn't. Dark curtains pooled in the window and crystals swung from colorful threads. The sign read SPELLS-BY-THE-SEA.

Bella spotted a blue-and-white shuttle-stop sign with a schedule printed on it. While they waited, Bram stood in the shade in front of the empty Snips-by-the-Sea hair salon.

"I don't think Casper can ride the shuttle," Cooper said, frowning. Casper sat, panting in the shadow created by the awning, clearly too hot to care that he was so close to Bram.

"In New York, people bring their pets on buses and subways all the time. They carry them." *Sometimes not that effectively,* she added to herself, remembering the giant brown-and-white Boxer wearing an oversized canvas tote bag on the subway. The owner had cut leg holes in the bag and hung onto the handles. "I'm sure it will be fine."

Bella hoped that her words were true.

To pass the time, Bella and Cooper pretended the cracks in the sidewalk were balance beams. Casper and Bram looked more and more uncomfortable as the sun shifted and their wedge of shade shrank. Finally, a small blue-and-white van arrived at the stop. As the door opened, the driver blew a pink chewing-gum bubble so big, it hid half his face.

"Does this bus go to the mall?" Bella asked, one foot on the stairs.

The bubble popped.

"It does. *That* doesn't." The driver pointed at Casper and inflated another bubble. "They make a mess on the floor and seats."

"But–" Bella started. The driver raised a hand, then sucked the bubble back into his mouth.

"Is it a therapy dog? Like a working dog?"

"N–no, but–"

"No buts." Another bubble.

Bella stood on the stairs, thinking hard. "What if we carry him?" she asked, thinking of the people in New York. "He won't be on the seat or the floor." She ignored Cooper tugging on the back of her shirt. "Please? It's just to the mall."

The bus driver blew another huge bubble. "Fine," he said, "but if there's a mess, you're cleaning it up."

"We will!" Bella said.

"This is *not* a good idea," Cooper whispered to Bella. He slipped his hands under Casper's belly and hoisted. Casper made a grumpy face.

Bella paid the driver for all four of them, then flopped into a seat next to Bram and across from Cooper, whose arms were wrapped around Casper's middle. Three other passengers rode the bus: two chatting ladies in the front and a man in the back who seemed to be asleep.

Bella let out a sigh. They'd made it.

"Today's the day!" she said, turning to Bram. "You'll get back to your family!"

Bram smiled at her with his pointy fangs, but his eyes were dull and his skin extra pale. "I am happy. And hungry. It was hot waiting."

"You'll get some food as soon as we get you to the mall," Bella reassured him. The bus pulled over at another stop, and the driver got out to use the wheelchair lift.

Bram leaned his head back and closed his eyes. A prickle of worry tickled Bella's neck. This was not good.

The wheelchair lift hummed.

"So ... thirsty." Bram groaned without opening his eyes. "Must turn, okay?"

Not a good idea, Bella thought. But before she could say anything—

POP!

The noise startled Casper, who started barking and wouldn't stop. Everyone on the bus turned to glare at them. Bram-bat hovered over the seat, mid-air.

"That's a *BAT!*" shrieked one of the ladies. "Get it *out!*"

The lady next to her screamed.

Cooper struggled to hang onto Casper, and the

dog jumped off his lap and onto the floor, his sharp barks filling the small shuttle. Bella wanted to plug her ears.

Bella leapt, attempting to capture Bram in her sweatshirt, but all the noise must have scared him. Instead of landing on the seat, he flew, swooping over the other riders' heads.

The two ladies rushed off the bus. The man in the back, now very much awake, swatted at Bram with a newspaper. "Get!" he shouted. He tripped and fell into the seat across the aisle. Bella turned to Cooper. "We gotta go!" she yelled over Casper's barks.

Cooper nodded and nudged Casper toward the front of the bus.

With one last throw, Bella tossed her sweatshirt over Bram-bat.

Got him!

"You'll get rabies!" the man with the newspaper shouted.

"I'll take my chances!" she called back, holding the bat bundle. She sprinted up the aisle on Cooper's and Casper's heels.

They jumped right over the stairs onto the sidewalk.

The driver climbed back into his seat, glaring at them. "You're never allowed on my shuttle again!" With the *sh* in *shuttle*, his bright pink gum flew out, splatting on the closed door.

Bella and Cooper watched, shocked, as the bus sped away.

At least Casper had finally stopped barking.

CHAPTER 15

Good Try

BELLA didn't want to look at Cooper, so she kept her back to him. What if he were mad? What if he left? She clutched the sweatshirt with Bram wrapped in it, heart pounding. How could they get Bram home now?

She took a breath, then turned to Cooper and Casper. The dog hung his head, as though ashamed of all his barking.

"Guess the shuttle is out," Cooper said, crossing his arms.

"We'll get there another way," Bella replied. But would they be able to? How? Hot rocks of despair filled her insides.

Cooper kicked at the sidewalk. "What do we do now?"

Bella tried to think. There weren't many options. Bram was still in bat mode, and she could tell by his closed eyes and rapid breathing that he wasn't doing so well. She wished her dad was here to give them advice. "Let's get Bram something to eat and then plan next steps."

"Fine," Cooper grumbled.

But it wasn't fine. As they trudged from the edge of town up Main Street, Bella realized that there wasn't any place that had what Bram needed. The stores that were open didn't have simple syrup or pancake syrup, and there were so many empty storefronts, they ran out of options quickly. Cooper didn't say much. The silence made Bella feel like she was wearing a pair of tight, uncomfortable shoes. What if he didn't want to be her friend anymore? Casper's tail hung down and his face drooped. Even he wasn't happy.

"We're near my house again," Cooper finally said. "Casper needs water. I'm gonna go home. We'll meet up later."

"Can you check and see if you have something for Bram?" she asked, worried.

Cooper nodded and they slowly turned down his street.

At the front steps, Casper pulled at his leash, tongue hanging out. Bella guessed that Bram would have his tongue out, too, if he were a dog. The little bat's eyes stayed closed.

"Wait here," Cooper said to Bella as Casper bounded up the stairs, tail swinging. He woofed at the closed door.

Cooper reached to open it when his brother appeared on the other side. Tall, wearing a deep frown, he blocked the doorway.

"Some of my candy's missing," DeShawn said, his voice rumbling. "I have a feeling I know who took it."

Cooper shrugged. "Why d'you think it was me? Let me in. Casper needs a drink."

"I know it was you, because none of the other guys like Pixy Pops. You owe me." He swung the door open. "Get in. You and your dog are with me for a while."

Bella had an idea.

"I . . . don't suppose you'd be willing to drop us off at the mall?" she asked.

DeShawn cocked an eyebrow at her over Cooper's head. "I don't suppose I would."

Cooper turned to Bella and shrugged. "Good try," he mouthed.

The door closed with a click of defeat. It was just Bella with Bram in the bundle in her arms.

"Let's go," she whispered to the bat, heart sinking even lower.

CHAPTER 16

Big Mushy Blob

WHEN they got home, Bella found a new bottle of maple syrup in Uncle Van's cabinet. Now Bram was snoozing in bat form under a shady bench in the garden.

That was perfect because Bella didn't want him to see her cry.

The tears poured down her face. Her insides felt like a big mushy blob of nothing-ever-works.

Was Cooper's brother really angry? Would Cooper and Casper be able to meet her later? What if they didn't want to?

She missed her old life, where there were no lost bat-boys or boys with dogs who barked at bat-boys. There were animal rescues and her friends and hot-dog carts. And her dad to talk with when she was upset.

Shiver-by-the-Sea was as gloomy and awful as its name.

Bella fished a crumpled tissue out of her shorts pocket and wiped the goo from her nose.

How could she get Bram home now? She didn't know enough about this place. It was so different from New York, where you could zip anywhere, anytime.

That made her think of their tiny apartment with her shoebox-sized bedroom that was too hot in the winter and their fire escape where Mom tried to grow tomato plants in the summer.

But no tomatoes grew.

And the faucet dripped unless you turned the

cold water off just right.

And the sirens wailed every day—and every night.

And her mom frowned for months, even before she lost her job.

A fat bumblebee flew by, looping lazily before landing on a bright pink flower. Bella's tears slowed.

In Shiver-by-the-Sea, her mom smiled.

The noise was from the chirping birds and Casper's barking.

The faucets didn't drip.

And she had a chance to help someone who needed her.

Bella wiped her eyes.

Shiver-by-the-Sea wasn't perfect, but there were good things about living here.

And good friends.

And, maybe, just enough magic.

CHAPTER 17

Best Uncle Ever

The sounds of clinking dishes and running water floated from the kitchen window. Uncle Van was home. Bella stood and stretched, then peeked under the bench. Bram was still asleep. Maybe Uncle Van could tell her some other way to get to the mall. Maybe things would be okay.

She followed a path past gnomes doing yoga to the sunny yellow back door. She took a deep breath, grasped the knob, and pushed.

Uncle Van wore shorts with all different colored stripes and a blue shirt. The bald spot on the back of his head shined in the light. Without turning he said, "Hey, Bells."

Uncle Van finished rinsing the plate and turned off the water.

"Thank you for your help," he said to the dish towel. The towel floated from his shoulder and hung itself neatly on the towel rack above the cabinet. She opened her mouth, surprised, and then shook her head, as if to clear it. *That's not the weirdest thing I've seen today.*

"How'd you know it was me?"

"No magic needed," he said to Bella. "I can see most of the back garden from this window." He turned to her with a worried expression. "And it seemed like you were not so happy in my garden. Want to talk about it?"

"Kind of," she said, but she didn't know how to start.

Uncle Van tilted his head. "Try," he said.

"Um, Uncle Van, I'm upset because . . . Can you help me figure out how to get to the mall? My friend Cooper and I tried to go, but they wouldn't let his dog on the shuttle. Is there another way to get there?"

Uncle Van frowned. "The mall? *Really?*"

Bella swallowed. "Yeah. It's . . . I'm sort of trying to find . . . something and they don't seem to have it in town." It was kind of a lie, but not really. She was trying to find the candy shop Bram's parents owned.

Uncle Van folded his arms. "You won't find what you want there," he said firmly.

"I think I will."

"What is it you're looking for?"

The too-tight, uncomfortable feeling came back. He was supposed to be telling her how to get there, not asking questions about what she wanted once she *got* there. "Um . . . some stuff. Is there another way?"

Uncle Van sighed and placed both hands on the

kitchen table, leaning toward her. "Look, Bella. I know kids like the mall. But it's ruined this town, and it's hard for me to think that you would want to spend time—and money—there. Especially since your mom is one of the people working to bring Shiver-by-the-Sea back. The mall . . . has no character. No personality. No magic."

It does have a family of vampire-bat people.

"I know," she said. "And I wouldn't go if it weren't super important. I need to be able to take Cooper and Casper and . . . another friend," she added, hoping a little more truth might work its own magic on her uncle. "So can you help?"

Uncle Van dropped his head and groaned. "Are you going to be there long? Is this one of those 'spend the whole day shopping' things kids do?"

"No way," Bella said, shaking her head. "I need to find one store, and that's it."

"With Cooper and a *dog*?"

Bella nodded. "Yeah."

Uncle Van straightened and tossed his hands in the air. "Fine. I'll drive you. But only because I'm the very best uncle who ever existed ever."

"You totally are," Bella said, grinning.

CHAPTER 18

A Tight Squeeze

An hour and a phone call promising to replenish DeShawn's Pixy Pops later, Cooper and Bella piled into the back seat of Uncle Van's tiny car. Casper filled in the hatchback, tail wagging and doggy breath fogging the window. The only thing the dog loved more than pickle chips was car rides. Uncle Van started the engine, then glanced over his shoulder.

"Okay, you need to have your bat friend turn into a kid to ride in my car. It's safer that way."

Bella's mouth dropped open. Cooper's, too. Casper's was already open—he was panting.

"What?" Bella said, sure she'd misheard.

"The bat. The one that likely ate my humming-bird food. The one wrapped in the sweatshirt that smells like maple syrup in your lap. He or she or they will turn into a human if asked nicely. You *do* know the bat turns into a person, right?" Uncle Van asked, raising his eyebrows.

Bella looked at Cooper. His mouth was still hanging open and his eyes were twice their normal size. Bella's felt about that big, too. She forced her own jaw closed, then swallowed. "You . . . know?"

Uncle Van chuckled. "I'm a magician, Bells. I grew up in Shiver-by-the-Sea. I know about all kinds of things, including that when you smell syrup and there's a bat around, it's likely able to turn into a person. And it needs a seat belt."

"I grew up here, too, and I didn't know any of this until two days ago!" Cooper said.

"The Shiver-by-the-Sea you've grown up in has a sliver of the magic it used to," Uncle Van responded. "But maybe things are changing."

Bella opened the car door and placed her sticky sweatshirt-wrapped Bram bundle in the grass next to the driveway.

POP!

Bram appeared, a bashful smile on his face.

"Slide over, you two," Uncle Van instructed. "It's going to be a tight squeeze."

CHAPTER 19

The Sweet Tooth

ON the ride to the mall, they told Uncle Van the whole story.

"Your family will be so glad to see you," he said as they walked in.

Cold air blew at Bella's face and goosebumps rose on her arms. The mall smelled like fried food and pretzels. Music blared from hidden speakers. She glanced at her uncle, whose brightly colored shorts appeared washed out in the harsh light. As a matter of fact, he seemed . . . colorless in general, like he could be anyone's uncle, not her magical one.

No magic here, she remembered. She got it now.

"I'm going to get a pretzel and wait on that bench for you guys," Uncle Van said. "Congratulations on finding your family," he said, turning to Bram.

"Thank you for your help," Bram said.

Casper tugged Cooper toward the pretzel stand.

"Not now," Cooper scolded. "I think we can find a list of the stores over there."

Bella and Bram followed Cooper across the concourse. Bella's heart thumped faster. They were going to get Bram home right in time for his dad's birthday!

They crowded in front of the mall map.

"What's the name of your parents' store?" Bella asked. Cooper pointed to the list of places under a header that read FOOD.

"Sweet Tooth," Bram said quietly.

"Found it!" Cooper pointed to the location on the map. "Down there, near the fountain. Let's go!"

They sprinted. Casper's legs pumped and he pulled the leash like he knew exactly where they were going, dragging Cooper along. Bella grabbed Bram's hand.

Up ahead, the fountain sparkled. A bunch of little kids stood at the edge, tossing coins into it.

Casper pulled to the left of the fountain, then stopped suddenly.

Bella almost crashed into Cooper. "What is it?" she panted.

Cooper pointed straight ahead.

A bright pink sign read THE SWEET TOOTH. The bottoms of the Ts in *tooth* were pointed to look like fangs.

Underneath the sign was a window with two bare white tables in it.

The store was dark as night.

And a big CLOSED—MOVING sign was taped to the door.

CHAPTER 20

Aaararrrrrr—ooooooohhhh!

BELLA felt like a punctured balloon. Her knees went weak and the hum of the mall's background noise seemed to fill her ears.

She turned to Bram, whose eyes were wet, then tightened her grip on his hand.

"Let's knock," she suggested. Making a fist, she banged against the glass. "Hello! Anyone home?"

They waited. Knocked again. One minute, then two. Casper snuffled at the bottom of the door, tail flinging back and forth.

"They are not there," Bram said quietly.

"Come on," Bella said, spotting a bench. She led him over and they all sat. Casper didn't get the message. He yanked at his leash, straining toward the Sweet Tooth.

"Don't you get it? No one's coming," Cooper scolded as he scooped up Casper and carried him to the bench. The dog's ears swung with each step, and he craned his neck to keep his eyes on the Sweet Tooth door.

"Bram, I'm sorry," Bella said, though she knew that the words wouldn't help. They'd tried so hard. "There has to be something else we can do."

Bram sat silent. He dropped his head to his hands, elbows on his knees. His shoulders shook.

Cooper and Casper plopped down on the other side of their friend. Over Bram's back, Bella and Cooper exchanged sad glances. Bella put her hand on Bram's shoulder. She didn't know what else to say.

Casper stuck his snout between the boy's face and hands and gave his cheek a big, sloppy lick.

Bella was surprised. "Usually, he doesn't want to be this close to Bram."

"He knows Bram's sad. He does that to cheer me up, too," Cooper said quietly.

As the three sat there, Bella's mind raced with possibilities: Go back and find Uncle Van? Could he help them? Maybe there was an office in the mall that would know where Bram's family went? Where would that be?

Finally, Bram straightened. Casper gave him the biggest lick yet—right up the whole front of his face. Bram laughed a little. "Okay, dog!"

Casper hopped down and snuffled under their bench.

"We'll figure something out," Bella said. "We can leave them a note. We'll keep looking till we find them."

Bram gave her a weak smile. "Maybe they *have* gone back to Transylvania."

"They wouldn't leave you," Cooper said. "I'm sure of it."

Bella nodded. "And we're not leaving you. Uncle Van knows about you now. You can stay with us while we look for your parents. You don't have to hide anymore." After a minute she added, "You're our family now. And family sticks together."

As soon as the words crossed her lips, Casper pushed her legs aside and bolted out from under the bench. His nose pointed straight at the ground, droopy ears almost blocking his face. He made a low *rowwrrrrr!* sound as he headed away from them, fast.

Cooper didn't have time to grab the leash. "Casper, wait!" he called. The three friends ran after the dog. "If he goes into a store, I'll get in so much trouble."

The end of the leash whipped along the floor, fast. Casper didn't pay attention to it, the crowd, or anything else. Shoppers dodged out of their way as the dog made a beeline to the Sweet Tooth. Casper stopped at the door, nose still down to the ground. His front paws scrabbled like he was digging a hole. Then, abruptly, he froze. Cooper managed to snag

the end of the leash just as Casper threw his head
back.

*AAaaahhhhhhhhhhhh-rrrrrrrrrrrr-
ooooooooooooohhhhhhhhhhhhhhhhhhh!!!!!!*

It was the biggest, loudest howl Bella had ever
heard.

*AAaaahhhhhhhhhhhh-rrrrrrrrrrrr-
ooooooooooooohhhhhhhhhhhhhhhhhhh!!!!!!*

Chills ran up and down her arms.

People stood stock-still. Conversations ended
mid-sentence. All eyes were on Bella, Cooper,
Bram, and the dog.

*AAaaahhhhhhhhhhhh-rrrrrrrrrrrr-
ooooooooooooohhhhhhhhhhhhhhhhhhh!!!!!!*

"Stop it!" Cooper pleaded. He dropped to the
ground next to Casper, eyes huge, then looked up at
Bella. "He's never done this before!"

As the words left Cooper's mouth, two things happened: the door to the Sweet Tooth swung open, and Bella spotted Uncle Van racing through the crowd, headed straight for them.

CHAPTER 21

Going Home

"**CASPER!**" Cooper called, but before he could stop him, the dog raced into the dark store, right past a pair of dark shoes.

"Papa!" Bram cried, throwing himself into the arms of the man attached to the legs of the feet in the dark shoes.

"Bella!" called Uncle Van, huffing and puffing as he caught up to them.

Bella waved, then followed Casper, Cooper, Bram's father, and Bram into the Sweet Tooth.

The store wasn't as dark as it had seemed from the outside. A small light glowed overhead. Casper was nose-first inside a bag of–Bella inhaled, *Of course!*–pickle-flavored potato chips.

Bram was wrapped tight in the arms of a tall

man who looked like an older version of him. "You came back to us!" the man cried.

Bram finally stepped out of the hug and faced his dad. "I am so sorry I left, Papa. I was scared and could not find my way home."

"Your mama and I were so worried about you.

We have been looking and looking, taking turns flying all day and all night." Dark under-eye shadows marred his pale skin. "She is flying now."

Bram gasped. "In the day?"

His father nodded.

Bella knew how hot and tiring it must be for Bram's parents to fly around in the sunlight. They loved him so much to do that.

"These friends helped me." He pointed at Cooper, Bella, and Uncle Van. "They got me here in time for your birthday."

"You are the best gift to me, Brammy." He turned to the group. "I am Abraham Orlok. I am happy to meet you and so glad you brought my son home." Bram looked like his father, only—Bella gulped—his dad's pointy teeth were much, much bigger.

"Why is the store closed?" Bram asked. "Where are you going?"

His father sighed.

"Sales were not good from the beginning. And then you left. . . . We thought we'd find you and go home to Transylvania. Family is more important than our business."

"No!" Bram said. "I made a mistake. I have friends now. I know you want to be here. We can stay."

Abraham's face fell. "I gave up the lease already. We cannot stay at the mall." He pointed to the pickle chips. "The people who helped us pack left those. They come back tomorrow to finish."

Bella cleared her throat. "I might have an idea. My mom's reopening the movie theater in Shiver-by-the-Sea. Movie theaters need candy. Maybe you can sell your candy there?"

"Trisha will go for it," Uncle Van said confidently.

Abraham rubbed his chin. "Maybe."

"I lived in the movie theater!" Bram said. "It is great!"

Everyone laughed.

Bram turned to Bella and Cooper. "Thank you," he said. "You got me home."

Bella's heart swelled. "You kind of got me home, too," she said.

CHAPTER 22

Opening Night

THE lights flickered.

"We have to get in our seats!" Bella said. She grabbed a box of chocolates and a small popcorn off the counter, then waved to Greta, Bram's mom, who was working the Sweet Tooth concession stand.

Cooper crossed the dark red carpet to the double doors.

"I'll be right there!" Bella called to him.

It was opening night of the Cinema Gosi, and the theater was packed. It seemed like everyone in town had come to see Uncle Van's magic act before the movie. He'd made two rabbits disappear and pulled a bouquet of flowers out of a lady's ear.

Bella weaved through the crowd, slipped through a door and up a flight of stairs to the projection room. Her mom was busy checking the reels on the old projector.

"Boo!" Bella cried, and her mom jumped.

"You scared me!" Mom said, laughing.

Bella handed her mom the popcorn. "Figured you'd want it for the movie."

Her mom took a handful and munched. "I can't believe we did it."

After getting Bram back to his family, the plan had worked: the Sweet Tooth moved into the movie theater. Between Bram's family, Uncle Van, Bella, and Cooper—with some help from DeShawn and Cooper's other brothers—they got the theater ready to open in time.

Watching all the people from town line up to buy tickets and congratulate her mom on reviving the old building made Bella burst with pride.

"I can believe it. You worked hard," Bella said.

Her mom gave her a hug. "Thanks for helping."

"I'm glad we did this, Mom."

"You mean opening the theater?" her mom asked, raising the Eyebrow.

"All of it," Bella answered honestly. "Moving here, opening the theater, living with Uncle Van, helping Bram. You were right: Shiver-by-the-Sea *is* a special place."

"In more ways than one, huh?" Her mom laughed. "Now go take your seat so I can start this thing!"

Bella blew her mom a kiss, headed out of the projection room, and followed the last of the crowd into the theater.

She spotted Cooper and Bram in the center and squeezed past some legs to join them. Bram had his fangs deep in an extra-large cup of soda syrup, and Cooper held the biggest popcorn tub Bella had ever seen.

"Ready?" she asked.

They nodded, grinning.

She settled in her seat, then looked around.

Shiver-by-the-Sea isn't strange, she thought. *It's magical. It's home.*

The lights went down, and the screen flickered to life.

Acknowledgments

Books are not created by one person. I am so grateful to the village of people who helped bring Bella's story to life:

Jennifer Laughran, my stellar agent, who believed in Bella, loved the kooky town of Shiver-by-the-Sea, and helped it find a home.

My critique group: Annette, Gary, Megan, Phoebe, and Wendy, who worked through my drafts with me and offered critical insight and suggestions through every step of the process.

My incredible editor, Alison Weiss, who embraced all that is Shiver-by-the-Sea, advocated tirelessly for this book, and helped shape Bella's story and world.

Awesome illustrator Jenn Harney, whose artwork perfectly captured the vibe of this quirky town and brought Cooper, Casper, and Bella to life.

Early readers Jesse Kahn, Anna Staniszewski, and Pam Vaughan, for taking the time to offer thoughtful feedback on the manuscript.

The entire team at Pixel+Ink, including publicist Bree Martinez, for getting excited about Bella's world and bringing Shiver-by-the-Sea to readers.

And I'm so grateful for my husband, Frank, and our kids, Charlotte and Harker—all of whom support me in my creative work, and each of whom contributed ideas and suggestions to make Shiver-by-the-Sea come to life. I love you more than you'll ever know.

PREPARE FOR MORE MONSTROUS FUN IN

ERIN DIONNE is the author of the Edgar Award-nominated *Moxie and the Art of Rule Breaking* as well as several other picture books and novels for middle grade and tween readers. She lives in Massachusetts with her family. Visit her online at ErinDionne.com.

JENN HARNEY is the author/illustrator of *Swim Swim Sink* and *Underwear!* and has illustrated many other beloved picture books and chapter books. She lives in Ohio with her family. Visit her online at JKHarney.blogspot.com.